Everyone Asked About You

Story by Theodore Faro Gross

Pictures by Sheila White Samton

Philomel Books ~ New York

for Ruth, always — TFG

for Claude — SWS

Nora, Nora, open the door,
Open the door, Nora Blue.

I came to say that at school today,
Everyone asked about you.

Ruth and Nellie asked,

    Mr. Petrocelli asked,

        Josh and Matthew, too –

Everyone asked about you!

Nora, Nora, open the door,
Open the door, Nora Blue.

I just came from the baseball game,
And everyone asked about you.

The pitcher asked,
  The slugger asked,
    All the outfielders, too —

Everyone asked about you!

Nora, Nora, open the door,
Open the door, Nora Blue.

I took a hike to the peak of Mt. Pike,
And everyone asked about you.

The porcupines asked,
    The mountain lions asked,
        The yellow butterflies, too —

Everyone asked about you!

Nora, Nora, open the door,

Open the door, Nora Blue.

I just explored the ocean floor,
And everyone asked about you.

The tortoises asked,

The sea horses asked,

A school of tuna, too —

Everyone asked about you!

Nora, Nora, open the door,
Open the door, Nora Blue.

I was hurled around the world,
And everyone asked about you.

The Swedes asked,

The Chinese asked,

East and West Africans, too!

Everyone asked about you!

Nora, Nora, open the door,

Open the door, Nora Blue.

I hitched a trip on a rocket ship,
And everyone asked about you.

The Man in the Moon asked,

A Martian platoon asked,

The Empress of Jupiter, too —

The whole universe asked about you!

All right, all right, Mister Sunshine Bright,
I've heard enough stories — no more!

If everyone really asked about me,
Why didn't they come to my door?

Text copyright © 1990 by Theodore Faro Gross. Illustrations copyright © 1990 Sheila White Samton.
All rights reserved. Published by Philomel Books, a division of The Putnam & Grosset Group,
200 Madison Avenue, New York, NY 10016. Published simultaneously in Canada.
Printed in Hong Kong by South China Printing Co. (1988) Ltd.
Book design by Nanette Stevenson. First Impression

Library of Congress Cataloging-in-Publication Data. Gross, Theodore Faro. Everyone asked about you
story by Theodore Faro Gross : pictures by Sheila White Samton. p. cm.
Summary: Nora's friend Charlie claims that everywhere he went in the universe they asked
about her, from the players at a baseball game to the Empress of Jupiter out in space.
ISBN 0-399-21727-4 [1. Stories in rhyme.] I. Samton, Sheila White. ill.
II. Title. PZ8.3.G913 Ev 1989 [E]—dc19 88-28131 CIP AC